Go-Cart Number 1

To Massi, who found a tiny frog in a pool full of splashing and shouting — E. M.

Please visit our web site at: www.garethstevens.com
For a free color catalog describing Gareth Stevens Publishing's list of high-quality
books and multimedia programs, call 1-800-542-2595 (USA) or 1-800-387-3178 (Canada).
Gareth Stevens Publishing's fax: (414) 332-3567.

Library of Congress Cataloging-in-Publication Data

Montanari, Eva.
    [Macchinina numero 1. English]
    Go-Cart number 1 / Eva Montanari.
      p. cm.
    Summary: George, a boy who loves riding in a car with his father,
enters a go-cart race and, in the process, learns to count to ten.
    ISBN 0-8368-4478-5 (lib. bdg.)
    ISBN 0-8368-4619-2 (softcover)
    [1. Carting—Fiction. 2. Automobile driving—Fiction. 3. Counting—Fiction.
4. Fathers and sons—Fiction.] I. Title: Go-cart number one. II. Title.
PZ7.M76344Go   2005
  [E]—dc22   2004056708

This edition first published in 2005 by
Gareth Stevens Publishing
A WRC Media Company
330 West Olive Street, Suite 100
Milwaukee, Wisconsin 53212 USA

This U.S. edition copyright © 2005
by Gareth Stevens, Inc. Original edition
copyright © 2003 by edizioni ARKA, Milan, Italy.
First published in 2003 as *La Macchinina numero 1*
by Edizioni Arka, Via R. Sanzio, 7-I-20149 Milano.

Gareth Stevens editor: Dorothy L. Gibbs
Gareth Stevens art direction: Tammy West

Printed in the United States
of America

1 2 3 4 5 6 7 8 9 09 08 07 06 05

Go-Cart Number 1

Eva Montanari

GARETH**STEVENS**

GS

PUBLISHING

A WRC Media Company

I like riding in the car with my dad.

Looking out my window, on the right-hand side of the car, I see the end of the road and the beginning of the sky. I see clouds floating high above and a bird flying past us — right through the red light!

Looking out his window, on the left-hand side of the car, my dad sees the traffic. He points out the old cars and the brand new ones and notices which cars go fast and which ones go slow.

I learn a lot when we're together — even though we see different things sometimes.

One afternoon when we were out for a ride, I leaned over toward Dad's window and pointed to a grasshopper. It was sitting at the bottom of a post — with its antennae sticking straight up!

Dad pointed to a sign at the top of the post. "Look, George," he said. "What does it say?" I asked. "There's going to be a go-cart race at the top of the hill, on Sunday," Dad said.

"Cart rentals at Pina's garage," he read out loud.

Go-Cart Race for Children
Sunday at 10:30 a.m.
at the top of the hill
Cart rentals at Pina's garage

"Come on," he said, "let's go rent one!"

At Pina's garage, we found go-carts of many different colors neatly arranged in the window. Each cart was in the shape of a number. Dad chose a red one in the shape of the number 1.

When we brought the cart home, my dad smiled and said triumphantly, "This go-cart is really a number 1."

Once we were inside, Dad pinned a long strip of paper
to the wall and started drawing on it. He drew a platform
that looked like a stairway. It had ten steps, with a number
under each step. It was the winner's platform, Dad told me.

We counted the steps together,
repeating the numbers again and
again. *"One, two, three, four,
five, six, seven, eight, nine, ten."*

Then Dad pointed to my place on
the platform. It was on the top step.
"With go-cart number 1," he said,
"you're sure to come in first!"

Early the next morning, we took
go-cart number 1 to the top of the hill.
Lots of children were there with their
number-shaped carts, and everyone
was ready to race.

When I heard the signal, I took off as
fast as I could. I wanted to come in first,
like my dad had said. Before I knew it,
my go-cart, number 1, was in the lead.

Looking out my window, on the
left-hand side of the cart, I saw a
little bird racing along with me.
After a while, the bird flew away.

Down the road, I saw *two* enormous cows.
They were blocking my way!

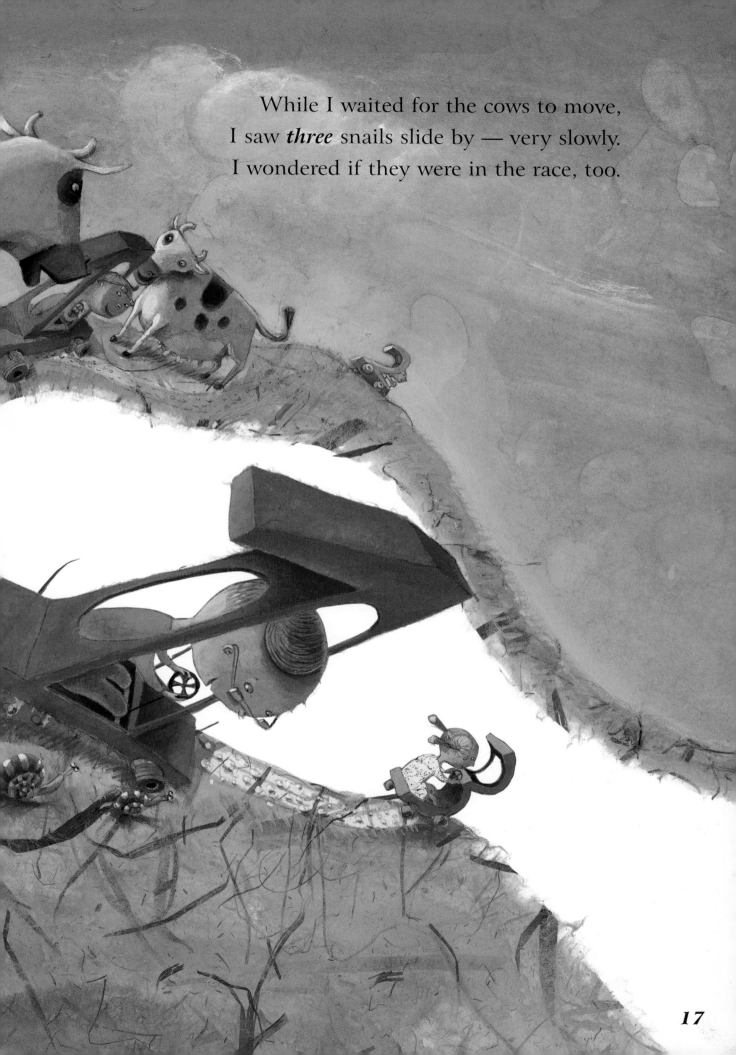

While I waited for the cows to move,
I saw *three* snails slide by — very slowly.
I wondered if they were in the race, too.

On my way again, I looked out my right-hand window and saw *four* sheep grazing. They never once lifted their heads. They were too busy nibbling grass to see me.

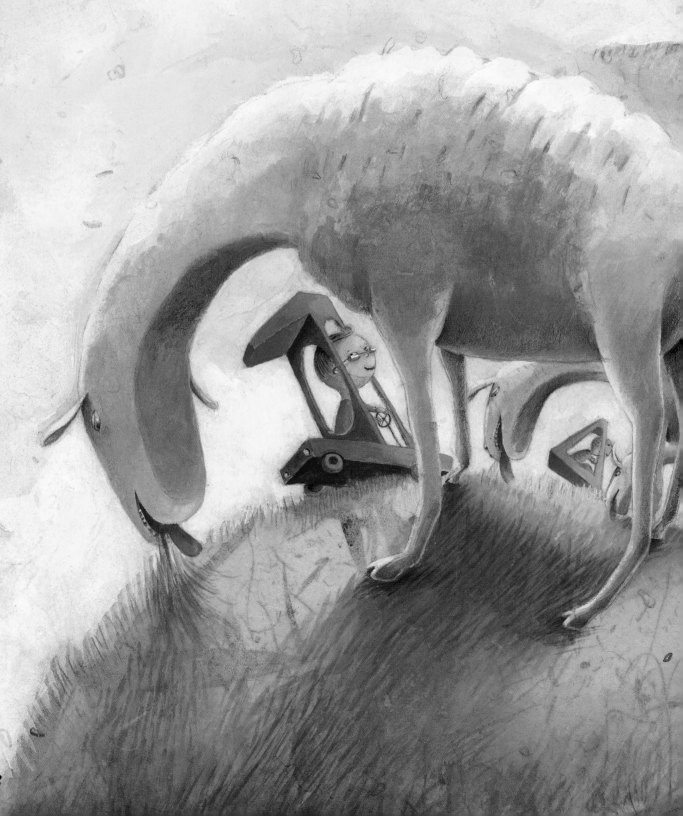

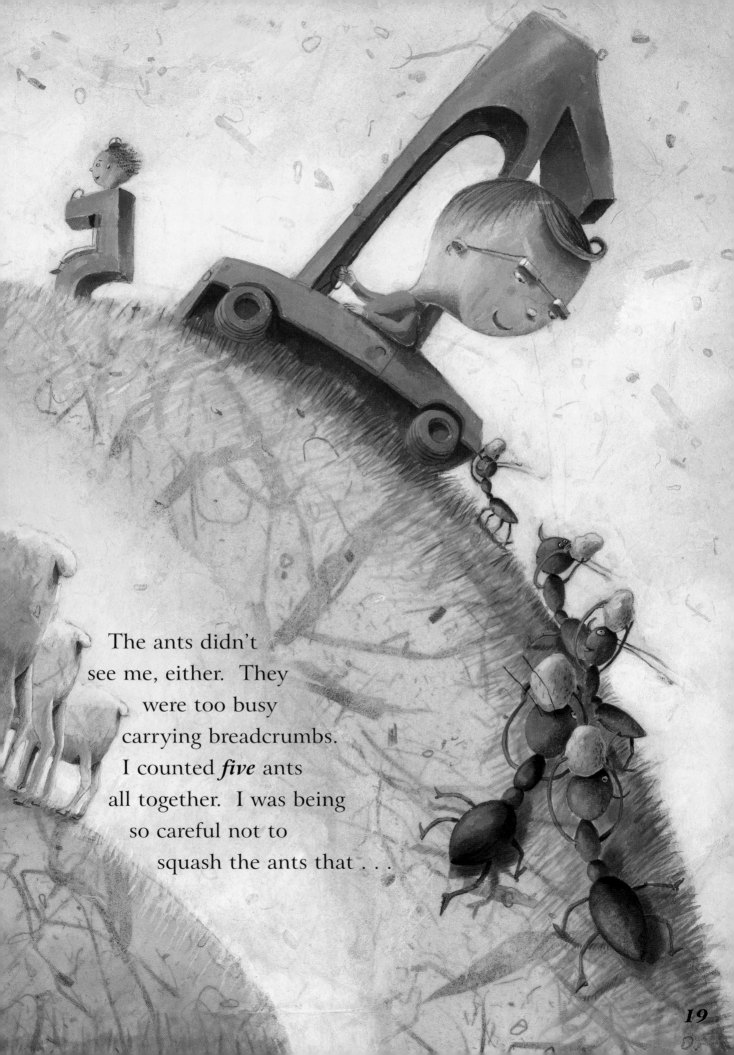

The ants didn't
see me, either. They
were too busy
carrying breadcrumbs.
I counted *five* ants
all together. I was being
so careful not to
squash the ants that . . .

I almost didn't see the honeybees. I heard them humming
as they flew by, and I counted **one**, **two**, **three**, **four**, **five**, **six**.
I wonder how much honey **six** bees can make.

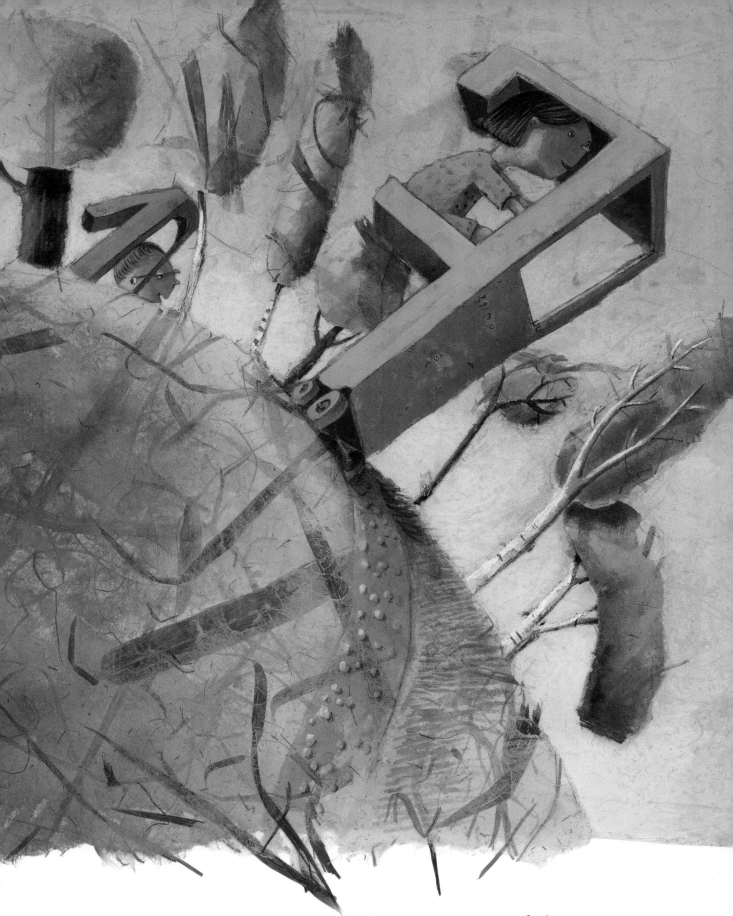

I saw some trees along the road, too — *seven* of them,
all in a line, with their top branches brushing the sky.

I drove on for quite some time, then looked out my right-hand window again. There, before my eyes, were *eight* beautiful sunflowers. I wanted to stop and pick them, but I couldn't because I was in a race.

Suddenly, I saw *one*, *two*, *three*, *four*, *five*, *six*, *seven*, *eight*, *nine*, *ten* brightly colored butterflies in front of me.

No, wait.

There were only *nine*.
The tenth wasn't a butterfly.
It was a girl riding in go-cart number 9.
She waved as number 9 passed me.

I'll have to go faster, I thought. I have to catch up with number 9 if I want to come in first.

The road climbed up and up. At the top, I discovered *ten* four-leaf clovers. I was about to get out of my go-cart to pick one for luck when I saw my dad. He was standing at the finish line — next to go-carts number 6, 7, 4, 5, 2, 3, 8, 9, and 10!

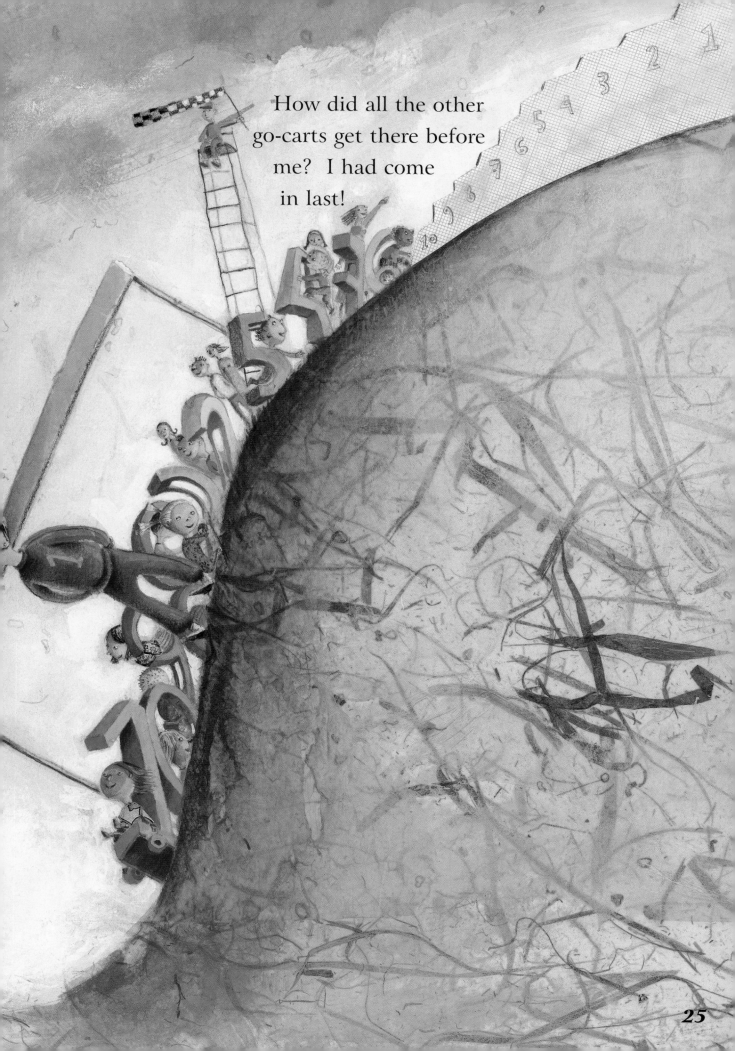

How did all the other
go-carts get there before
me? I had come
in last!

I took my place on the winner's platform.
It was just like the platform Dad had drawn, except
my place was on the bottom step, instead of on the top step.
I was tenth instead of first — but everyone got a prize!

The prize for first place was a helicopter with **one** propeller.
The second-place prize was a **two**-wheeled scooter. The prize
for third place was a doll with **three** outfits; for fourth
place, a soldier with **four** horses; and for fifth place,
a toy train with **five** cars.

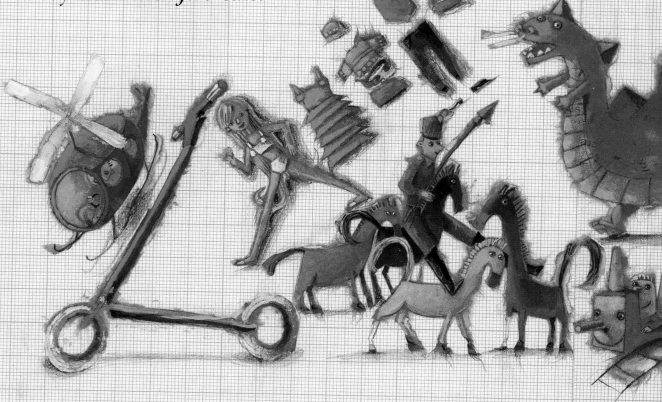

The prize for sixth place was a dragon with *six* spiky crests. For seventh place, it was a building set with *seven* snap-together blocks. A puzzle with *eight* pieces was the prize for eighth place, and a space-alien doll with *nine* eyes was for ninth. Finally, a strange wooden object with *ten* balls on metal rods was handed to the tenth-place driver — me!

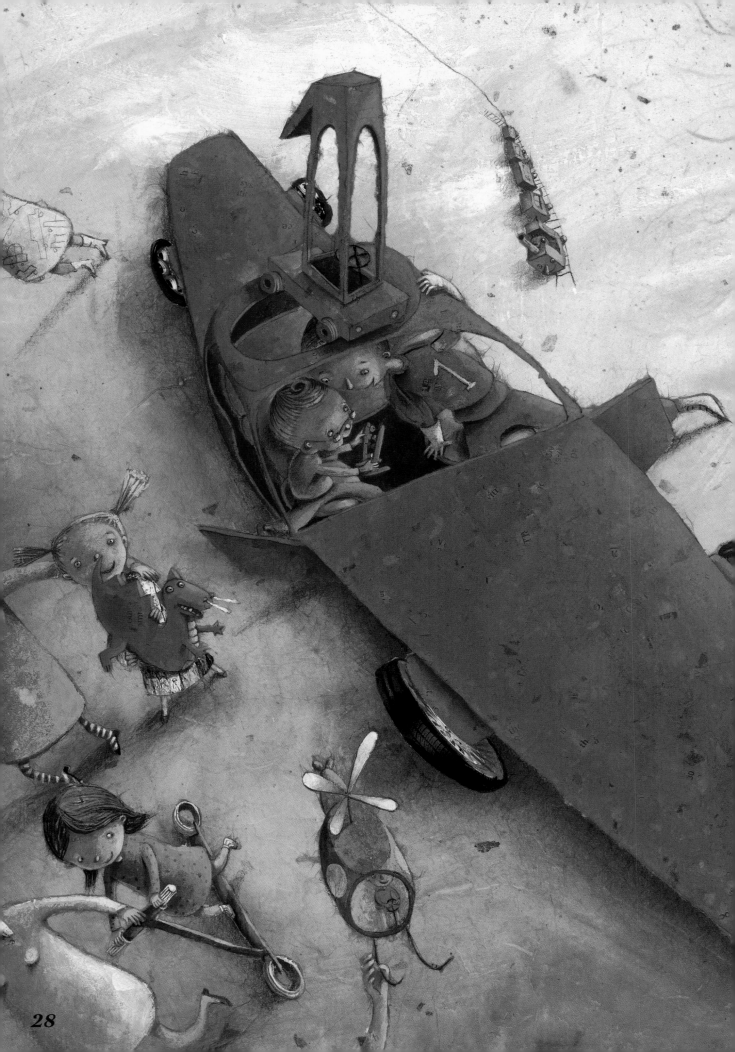

"What is this?" I asked my dad as we got into the car to drive home.

"An abacus," he replied. "It's for learning to count to ten."

"Then I don't need it." I said proudly. "I already know how to count to ten!"

"And you know what else, Dad?" I said. "During the race, I saw *one* little bird, *two* enormous cows, *three* very slow snails, *four* sheep eating grass, *five* ants carrying breadcrumbs, *six* humming honeybees, *seven* tall trees that were all in a line, *eight* beautiful sunflowers, *nine* brightly colored butterflies, and *ten* four-leaf clovers."

Dad was smiling. He wasn't upset at all that I didn't come in first.

"Look, George!" Dad said suddenly. He was
pointing out the window on his side of the car.

"I see a grasshopper sitting on the side mirror — with its antennae sticking straight up!"

I think Dad likes riding in the car with me. We see different things, sometimes, but we learn a lot when we're together.